The Preacher's Wife
By Jennie May

The Preacher's Wife

ISBN 978-0-557-76154-8

Chapter One

Frankie sat perched on the wooden chair outside of the farmhouse's front room that Nick used as his office. She and Nick had been married for only a few months, and he had recently begun a position as pastor of the nearby Abington Community Church. Nick was handling the position well, in spite of those who thought he was too young for that level of responsibility. He had proven that he had the experience and the skills to lead the church effectively as well as to deliver inspiring and enlightening sermons. Frankie, however, was finding that her role as a pastor's wife was not as easy as she had expected. In spite of years watching her mother in the same role, Frankie was having trouble with the diplomacy and grace required.

Frankie couldn't see into the office, but she was still aware of the unfolding events. The door was open, and she could hear everything that was happening inside. She bit her lip, listening to the conversation.

"I understand," said Nick. His voice was low, serious and completely professional.

"It's not that we necessarily disagree with what Frankie said," a higher voice explained nervously. "We understand her feelings on the matter."

"But we disagree with the tone she took with Mrs. Dell and with the words that she used to explain her position," said Marshall Kent, the oldest and most serious member of the church board. Frankie could just picture the old man's round face crumpled into concern.

"I understand completely," Nick repeated. "Frankie needs to learn how and when to express herself."

Frankie winced. She felt terrible that she had put her husband in this position. He had just started his job, and she was already causing trouble. She had known all along that Mrs. Dell had been one of the people who had been against Nick's being hired as pastor.

Frankie thought about Mrs. Dell and tried to contain a grumble. Old Mrs. Dell was the most miserable woman in the church. She complained about everything from Nick's sermons to the color they had painted the church nursery. She had been talking Frankie's ear off last Sunday when she mentioned that she didn't believe children under the age of 5 should even be brought to church.

"Disruptive, that's what they are," the woman had said, squinting her eyes at a group of children playing nearby. "In my day, children knew how to behave. Now they just run like wild animals. You should speak to your husband about banning children from services."

"Banning the children?" Frankie had repeated. "But how will they know about God?"

"They'll find out about God when they're old enough not to both me during worship," Mrs. Dell had snapped.

For a moment Frankie had just stood in front of the woman, shocked. Then, too quickly, she found her voice.

"Jesus said let the little children come to me. Perhaps we should ban nasty old women instead, Mrs. Dell."

As soon as the words left her mouth, Frankie wished she could grab them all and shove them back in.

Mrs. Dell had huffed and turned quickly on one heel. Then she'd made a beeline for Marshall Kent.

That was why the church board was visiting Nick today. Frankie was so embarrassed she felt like crawling under a table. But she knew that if she wasn't there to see the church board to the door, it would disappoint Nick.

She would do her duty as a minister's wife, even if it squashed her pride.

Frankie stood as the little group left Nick's office. She stood with her hands clasped against the back of her skirt and forced a smile.

"I'm glad you understand, Nick," Marshall Kent said, shaking her husband's hand.

Nick nodded solemnly. "I'll take care of it Marshall. I appreciate you bringing it to my attention."

Frankie swallowed hard. She moved to stand beside her husband and say goodbye to the church board as they left the little house. Each member told Frankie goodbye, but each seemed a little bit nervous to be speaking to her. Frankie felt like a naughty child who had been tattled on by the neighbors.

Nick closed the door and turned the lock with a click. Then he settled his eyes on Frankie. He raised his eyebrows. “You have anything to say for yourself?”

She shook her head. “There’s no excuse. I shouldn’t have said it. She just made me so mad.”

Nick titled Frankie’s chin up to his face and kissed her gently. “I love your passion, baby. But you know that being a minister’s wife calls for an exceptional level of self-control.”

“I know,” she answered softly. “I’m sorry, Nicky.”

He nodded and kissed her again. “You know I can’t let this go.”

She felt anxiety bubbling up inside her. “I know.”

Nick sighed. “Go upstairs. I’ll be right up.”

Frankie turned and climbed the creaky steps of the farmhouse. She dreaded what she knew was coming. She realized that she deserved a spanking, not for her opinion but for the way she had voiced her opinion. She and Nick had talked at length about whether Frankie felt that she was ready for the responsibility of being the minister’s wife. Frankie knew that she could be outspoken and opinionated but that a minister's wife should be kind and considerate of the members of the congregation. She had seen her mother hold her tongue a thousand times as the minister's wife at the church where Frankie grew up. Frankie had let her anger get the best of her when speaking to Mrs. Dell and that was simply not okay. Her mother would never have let that happen, and Frankie was determined to set higher standards for herself in the future.

When she reached the bedroom, she sat down on the old lace comforter her parents had given her. She looked around her bedroom, the room she thought of as her grown-up married room. The bedroom was filled with antiques and romantic décor. Frankie loved everything about it from the design of soft roses on the rug to the lace curtains on the window. Everything about the intimate space they shared reminded Frankie of the love between herself and her husband.

It was only a few minutes before Nick opened the door. He sat beside his wife on the bed, his larger frame denting the mattress and pulling her toward him. He turned to her.

"You know I don't fault you for your opinion," he said.

She nodded. "I know."

"And you know I am aware that some members of the congregation can be very difficult."

She nodded again. "Yes. But I still should never have said what I did."

"That is true." Nick folded his hands and looked thoughtful. "I'm going to tell you something that I probably shouldn't."

Frankie titled her head. He had gotten her attention.

"You know that I can't share what members of the congregation have told me in confidence," he said. "But this is a story I heard from another member, so I feel that it's okay to tell you."

She nodded again, wondering what he could be talking about.

He looked at her sternly. "But you will not repeat this. That would be gossip, you understand me?"

She bobbed her head up and down. "You can trust me."

"I know I can, baby" he said. He smiled at her. "Mrs. Dell has been a member of Abington for more than 60 years."

"Wow," said Frankie, impressed. "That's a long time."

"She became a member of the congregation when she married her husband. He died about 15 years ago."

Frankie listened, trying to imagine Mrs. Dell as a young bride. All she could picture was that wrinkled, angry face on someone in a bridal gown.

"Mr. and Mrs. Dell wanted children very much, but they were only able to have one. That child died before his first birthday."

Frankie's heart dropped. Tears began to gather in her eyes. "That's so sad," she whispered.

"Yes," Nick agreed. "And that could be the reason that children bother her. It could just be that it hurts her terribly to watch them."

Frankie wiped the moisture from her eyes as Nick continued.

"Honey, you don't know what's in people's hearts. That's why you have to be gentle. We all make mistakes based on ways we've been hurt. You can't judge others because you don't know their stories."

Frankie felt a hole in her heart. She knew that Nick was right. It wasn't fair of her to judge Mrs. Dell for her rants. She didn't know where that pain had come from.

"I can tell that you're sorry for what you said," Nick told her gently. "I'm still going to spank you, though, just to help you remember that you are the wife of a minister."

Frankie bit her lip and looked down at the bed.

Nick pulled her across his lap and positioned her bottom over his thighs. Then he flipped up her skirt and pulled down her panties.

"You have more responsibilities than the average woman, Frankie," he told her sternly. "You are a minister's wife, and the way you act is a reflection of me."

Frankie felt chastised before the spanking even started. When it did start, the stinging slaps fell fast and with force. Her bottom soon felt like a ball of rubber left out in the sun. She involuntarily kicked her feet and closed her eyes tightly as Nick's hand landed again and again on her bare cheeks.

The spanking wasn't long, but the sting in Frankie's bottom was intense when Nick let her up. There were tears in her eyes as she stood in front of her husband.

"I love you," Nick told her, his eyes revealing his adoration. "I don't know what I'd be without you. I know that I ask a lot from you so that I can pursue my calling, and I appreciate that you are willing to fill that role."

"Of course I'm willing!" Frankie said, momentarily forgetting the sting in her backside. She threw her arms around him. "My calling is to support you in yours. I'll do better, Nick. I promise."

He laughed, pulling her onto his lap. She winced as she sat. "Maybe you'd better promise to try."

"I promise to try," Frankie told him. She kissed him and snuggled into his shoulder, breathing in his scent.

He held her there for a moment and then let his hands began to wander over her body. Frankie groaned and pushed herself toward him.

They both stayed in the bedroom until the next morning.

Chapter 2

Frankie put on a green dress for Wednesday night Bible study and twirled in front of the mirror. She liked the old-fashioned look of the pleated skirt. She felt pretty but in a mature, grown-up way in the clothing. She knew that Nick liked her to wear modest and feminine clothing, and she had found in the few months they'd been married that she liked it too.

"Frankie!" Frankie heard Jessica's voice floating up the stairs.

"Come on up, Jess!" she called.

Frankie's best friend opened the bedroom door a few minutes later. "Oh, I love the dress!" said Jess.

Frankie smiled. "Mom made it. She likes me in green."

Jessica nodded her approval. "You do look great in green, especially that bright color. Maybe I should consider green as a wedding color? I've been thinking about it."

Frankie turned to her friend with a gleeful grin. "So how are the wedding plans coming?"

Jessica was engaged to Frankie's older brother, Josh. Frankie couldn't wait to be the Matron of Honor at their wedding.

Jessica smiled. "It's going okay."

Frankie looked concerned at the tone of Jessica's voice. "Is everything alright between you and Josh? You don't sound very happy."

Jessica's smile widened. "I'm deliriously happy. We're just going through a time where we have some things to work out."

Frankie nodded. She wanted desperately to ask what those things were, but she knew that Jess would tell if her if she wanted her to know. She waited a few minutes to see if Jessica would spill any details, but her friend remained silent.

"You'll let me know if you need anything?" Frankie said finally.

Jessica nodded. "Of course I will. And how about you? Are you ready for the big apology tonight?"

Frankie groaned and flopped onto the bed. Nick had told her that she needed to apologize to Mrs. Dell at the Bible study that evening. "I am not looking forward to that."

“Just say you’re sorry and then get away from her,” Jessica advised. “Make it as quick as you can.”

“I’ll do my best,” said Frankie. She picked herself up off the bed. “We’d better get going. Nick won’t want to be late.”

Jessica followed Frankie down the stairs. Nick and Josh were sitting at the kitchen table, talking in hushed voices. They stopped when the women entered the room.

“Talking about us?” Frankie teased.

Josh greeting Frankie with a smile and then took Jessica’s hand. “Are you ready, hon?”

Nick stood and kissed his wife. “You look adorable.”

“And contrite,” Josh teased.

Frankie glared at her older brother. It was just like him to tease her about having to apologize.

“We’re taking two cars,” Nick said to Frankie. “Are you okay to drive home by yourself so that I can stay and have a meeting?”

Frankie was confused. “Why can’t Josh and Jess bring me home?”

“The meeting is with them,” Nick said casually.

Frankie looked at Jess, but she was looking at Josh. It was then that Frankie began to realize that the three of them were keeping something from her. She felt anger rise inside. It wasn't fair of them to have a big secret.

"I can drive home," she said, a hint of anger in her voice.

Nick's eyebrows rose slightly but all he said was, "You know you can call me if you have any trouble."

Frankie followed Nick to their old sedan while Josh and Jess got into Josh's black coupe.

Nick opened the door for Frankie and then slid into the driver's seat. Frankie tapped the rubber mats on the floor in front of her, interested in how they felt in her new flats. The car's dirty floor reminded her of her father's truck when she was a little girl. There had been a small hole in the floor, and Frankie had liked to watch the road go by underneath her feet.

"What are you meeting Josh and Jess about?" she asked innocently. She knew he wouldn't tell her, but she thought it was worth a try.

"I am counseling Josh and Jess," he told her. His voice was firm. "It's part of my job as their pastor."

Frankie wrinkled her nose. "Like pre-marital counseling?"

"You know I can't tell you that," Nick said. "What is discussed between a pastor and members of the congregation is not to be shared."

Frankie huffed. "But this is my best friend and my brother!"

Nick shook his head. "Frankie, you knew from the beginning that there were going to be times when I couldn't share details of my job with you. This is one of those times, and I expect you to be an adult about this. Josh and Jessica have already said they don't want anyone to know."

So no one was going to tell her. Frankie felt like someone had stuck a knife into her gut. She folded her arms over her chest, trying not to cry. Three of the closest people in her life were keeping a secret, shutting her out. She turned and looked out the window for the rest of the drive.

It was a clear, cool evening and the Bible study was full. The men were meeting in the sanctuary while the women met in the conference room. Children and youth had their own Bible studies in the Sunday School wing of the large church.

Frankie met Jessica in the parking lot and walked with her to the women's Bible study area where they were the first to arrive. Jessica put her Bible and notebook down in front of one of the chairs and looked out the window.

"She's here," said Jessica after a minute.

Frankie followed Jessica's glance. Through the window she saw Mrs. Dell walking up the path in her ugly, sensible shoes and her little old lady dress with a large flower pattern that made Mrs. Dell look lost inside it. Frankie tried to see the grieving mother in the old woman's face, but it was hard to get past that reproachful look.

As Mrs. Dell made her way into the church, a few other women began to trickle into the room and take their seats. Frankie greeted each one with a smile and a question about their families or lives. When Mrs. Dell entered the room, she didn't even give Frankie a chance to say hello.

"I understand you have something to say to me," Mrs. Dell said sharply.

Frankie felt her face grow warm, and the other women looked away. Everyone had heard the story about Frankie and Mrs. Dell.

"Um," Frankie stammered. "Let's go into the hall."

Mrs. Dell turned and stepped into the hallway. Frankie followed and shut the door.

"I would think you could give me your apology in front of the other women," Mrs. Dell scolded.

"I thought it was a private matter," said Frankie softly.

"I told them they should never have hired such a young minister. Your husband is simply too young to lead a congregation. How can he lead this church when he cannot even control his wife?" Mrs. Dell ranted loudly. Frankie knew every woman in the Bible study room could hear her. She moved a few steps away from the door, willing herself to stay under control.

Frankie could feel her cheeks blazing with embarrassment and anger. She tried to keep her voice calm. "My husband is an excellent minister. Please don't blame him for my failings."

"I certainly do blame him," Mrs. Dell said. "You are to submit to your husband, and he is to lead you. Young people get married today with no understanding of God's will in marriage."

Frankie closed her eyes and mentally counted to ten. "Mrs. Dell, I am sorry for what I said to you last Sunday. I should not have said it, and I apologize."

Mrs. Dell pursed her lips. "You have no respect for your elders and no sense of decency. I told the church board that your husband has no business leading this congregation when his wife is such a foolish and undisciplined girl. I told them that they should be looking for another pastor immediately."

Frankie breathed deeply. "My husband is an excellent pastor and will serve this congregation with his whole heart. Shall we go into Bible study now?"

"Your husband is nothing more than an immature child. If he were a real man, he would take you in hand," Mrs. Dell said, brushing past Frankie and opening the door to the conference room.

"My husband is more man than you've ever known in your life, you miserable old biddy!" Frankie shouted after her. She put a hand to her mouth as she heard each woman in the Bible study group gasp. Jessica was standing with her mouth hanging open.

Mrs. Dell wheeled around. Frankie thought she saw fire in the old woman's eyes. "I will be speaking to Marshall about this right now, and your husband can kiss his job good-bye."

Mrs. Dell stomped out of the room. Frankie and the rest of the women watched her go.

It was Jessica who broke the silence. “It’s okay, Frankie. Mrs. Dell is just a hateful woman. You held your temper as long as you could.”

The other women murmured in agreement.

“Delilah Dell has always been sharp tongued,” said Mrs. Hatcher, who was nearly as old as Mrs. Dell. “She’s been causing trouble since long before you and your husband came to this church.”

“That woman could try the patience of a saint,” said Laura Jones, a young mother of three, pregnant with her fourth.

Frankie sank into a chair and shook her head. “No. I should not have lost my temper, no matter what Mrs. Dell said to me. It wasn’t right.”

“You’re only human,” said Annie Brinkman gently. Annie was leading the Bible study. “Let’s open our Bibles and try to forget this unpleasant episode.”

Frankie knew that Nick would be over to have a word with her before beginning his meeting with Jessica and Josh. She wasn’t surprised when he stepped into the room at the end of the Bible study and led a closing prayer before watching the women leave the room one by one. Annie was last to leave, and Nick shut the door behind her.

He took a seat across the table from his wife. "You want to tell me what happened?"

Frankie blinked back tears. "She just… she just made me so angry, Nick. She said that you shouldn't be leading this congregation and that we didn't know what a marriage should be and that you can't control your wife."

Nick nodded. "Well, she appears to be right about that last part."

Frankie burst into tears. "And now you're going to lose your job, and it's all my fault!"

Nick went to his wife and held her against him for a moment. Then he placed her at arm's length so he could look into her eyes. "You have not cost me my job. Every person on the board knows that Mrs. Dell is difficult, and there is no chance that they are going to ask me to leave."

Frankie sniffed. "Really?"

"Really," said Nick. "And I don't care about all that. God has placed me in this church for a reason. When He is ready to place me somewhere else, then it will be time to go."

Frankie nodded. She knew it was true.

"However, you are what I am concerned about," Nick told her.

Frankie sighed. "I'm sorry. I really am. I was sorry the second it happened."

"I'm not doubting your sincerity, honey. I know that you're sorry. But this is something that you have to get under control," Nick told her. "You are going to run into difficult people in this world, and you are going to have to learn to deal with them without losing your temper."

"I know," Frankie whispered.

Nick stood and kissed her hair. "Jess and Josh are waiting in my office, but we'll discuss this when I get home."

He kissed her on the forehead. "You sure you're okay to drive home alone?"

She nodded.

"Okay. I'll be there in an hour or so. Be in the bedroom."

He opened the door for her and then watched her walk down the path to the car before turning in the direction of his office.

When Frankie got home she fixed herself a cup of tea and went upstairs to change into a white nightgown. She sat for a while, considering what she had done and why. Then she reached for the phone and dialed her mother's number.

"Hello Frankie," her mother's voice was cheerful. "Nice to hear from you, dear."

"Hi Mom," Frankie said, the sound of her mother's cadence and familiar tone was reassuring. She cradled the phone against her cheek.

"Honey, what's wrong?"

Frankie laughed. Bobbi Jo always knew when something was wrong just from the sound of Frankie's voice.

"I'm having some trouble controlling my temper," Frankie admitted.

"Uh oh," said her mother. "Are you and Nick fighting?"

"No, it's not Nick. It's a woman at church."

"That's even worse," her mother said bluntly. "What's going on?"

"I said some really awful stuff to her," Frankie said. "She just makes me so mad and I don't know how to control myself."

"What does Nick say?" her mother asked.

"He says to control my temper," Frankie said with a chuckle. "I'm trying, but I guess I just don't know how."

"Sometimes when I had trouble with church members, I would write them terrible letters," said Bobbi Jo.

"You did?" Frankie was very surprised.

"Then I would destroy them, of course," said her mother quickly. "But it did help me hold my tongue."

"That's not a bad idea," said Frankie thoughtfully.

"And there's always that old piece of advice to not say anything if you don't have something nice to say. It's better to have people think the cat's got your tongue than have angry words spill out."

Frankie felt better. That was good advice. "I think I need to wire my mouth shut."

"Just pretend the wires are there, honey," said her mom. "Church members can be very difficult, but it's your job to be kind to them all."

"I know, Mom. Thanks," Frankie said. She heard the lock downstairs. "Nick's home. I should go."

"Goodnight, Frankie," said her mom. "It will work out."

Frankie hung up the phone and listened to the sounds of Nick relocking the door and putting his things away. She heard him coming up the stairs, and she tensed.

When Nick came into the room, he was holding a small wooden paddle. Frankie felt a knot in her stomach.

"You and I are going to figure this out," Nick announced.

Frankie looked up at him from the bed but didn't say a word. He was still dressed in a long-sleeved shirt and black pants. She noticed he had taken off his tie. He stood over her, his face serious.

"I've been thinking a lot about this, Frankie, and I think you can do a lot better. I know that Mrs. Dell makes you angry, but that is a very childish excuse for being rude to her," Nick said. He folded his hands across his chest, the paddle firm in his right hand.

"I've been understanding about this," he continued. "But I realized tonight that I wouldn't even accept this behavior from a child. The problem is one of self-control."

Frankie felt her toes curl. She knew he was right.

"That's why I'm going to paddle your bottom," Nick told her. "I expect you to control yourself. You obviously don't have enough reasons to exhibit self-control, so I'm going to give you another one. Get up."

Frankie crawled out of the bed and stood in front of her husband.

"I expect you to hold your temper," Nick told her. "Do you understand me?"

Frankie nodded. She already had tears in her eyes.

"You need to understand when it is not appropriate to say whatever pops into your head," he told her. "Every time I hear you speak rudely to someone, no matter the reason, I'm going to paddle your bottom. You understand?"

"Yes sir," Frankie replied softly.

Nick took Frankie's shoulders and gently turned her toward the bed. Then he bent her over the side so that her bottom was hanging off the edge and her feet dangled to the floor.

Nick pushed her nightgown up to her waist and pulled her panties down around her knees.

"I don't want to have to discipline you for this again," he told her.

Frankie squeaked when the paddle hit her bottom square in the middle. She realized that he wasn't going to start slow as he sometimes did when he wanted her to remember to behave herself. This spanking wasn't just a reminder. This was discipline, and Nick intended her to feel it from beginning to end.

Nick was not using the paddle to pop her bottom randomly as he usually did. Instead he was aiming hard swats low and in the center of her bottom. Each time the paddle landed she was thrust forward onto the bed. Each painful swat built on the one before.

Frankie started to cry when she realized that she had no idea how long Nick intended to keep spanking her and that her bottom was red and raw. She knew she would feel this spanking for days every time she attempted to sit.

“I’m sorry,” she said through her tears. “I won’t lose my temper, Nicky. Please.”

“This childishness stops now,” Nick told her. He smacked her hard again, and she yelled. She was feeling ashamed of herself, and her tears began to spill uncontrollably.

“I’m sorry!” she repeated.

Nick finished the spanking with five hard swats that nearly had her jumping up off the bed. When he was finished, he pulled her to standing.

He sat on the bed and placed her between his knees. Then he spun her around for a look at her bottom.

Frankie was still crying, but softly.

"Your bottom is bright red," he told her. "Every time you sit down and feel that tender behind, I want you to remember what I expect from you."

He turned her back around to face him.

"I'm serious, Frankie. Once was an accident, but twice is out of control. You are a grown woman, and you can control your temper."

"Yes sir," she whispered, sniffling.

Nick helped Frankie step out of her panties and then sent her into the bathroom to wash her face. When she returned, he was getting ready for bed.

"I'm sorry, Nicky," she said again. "Really."

He sighed and then smiled at her. "Don't make me do this again."

She shook her head. "I won't. I promise I won't."

She crawled into bed, her bottom sore against the sheets, and waited for him to turn out the light. She was thoroughly ashamed of her behavior but ready to control herself in the future.

Chapter 3

They had been in there a long time. Frankie stood outside the closed door of Nick's office wondering what the three of them were talking about. She could hear the high pitch of Jessica's voice and the low tones of her brother's, but she couldn't understand the words.

Frankie knew that if Nick saw her standing in the hallway attempting to eavesdrop he would be furious. That was why she listened especially hard for footsteps signaling that someone was coming to open the door.

Jessica's voice sounded upset, like she was about to cry. Josh's was comforting.

What could they be talking about? Frankie's curiosity was making her crazy.

Carefully she moved closer to the door. Slowly she moved her head so that her ear could rest against the wood.

"Brrrrring!"

The sound of the phone startled her, and she jumped. She froze for a moment to make sure that no one inside had heard her, but the voices didn't pause in their conversation.

Frankie headed to the kitchen to grab the phone. The caller ID showed that it was her sister, Evie. Evie was only a year older than Frankie, and the sisters had always been close.

"Evie!" Frankie exclaimed when she answered.

Evie's voice was soft and clear, just as it had always been. "Hi Frankie. What are you up to?"

Frankie almost blushed and did not admit what she had just been up to. "Oh nothing. Cleaning up a little and then checking on some church stuff for Nick. You?"

Evie sighed. "Same old. I was thinking about taking a break."

"Are you at work? Have some lunch," Frankie suggested.

Evie laughed. "I am at work but that wasn't the kind of break I was talking about. I was thinking about coming to visit you and Nick. Is it long enough since the honeymoon that I can visit?"

Frankie smiled and leaned against the kitchen cabinet, ecstatic about the idea of a visit from her sister. "Silly, Evie! Yes, of course you can visit. You are always welcome. When are you coming?"

There was a pause on the other end of the phone and then the answer. "Tomorrow?"

Frankie was surprised but not unhappy. "Great! Tomorrow it is. I'll fix up the guest room in the morning."

"Thanks," Evie said. Frankie thought she detected a sigh in her sister's voice.

"Are you okay, Evie?"

"I'm fine," her sister assured her. "I just want to come see what married life is doing to you."

Frankie laughed. "Well, I hope it's mostly good!"

"My little sister, good? Doubt that," Evie replied. "I do have to go back to work, but I'll see you tomorrow?"

"Tomorrow," said Frankie. "Bye!"

"Bye!" Evie was gone with a click.

Frankie laughed with joy. She would love a visit from her sister, and having Evie around would keep her mind off of whatever was going on with Jessica and Josh.

Jess and Josh were both looking very serious when they left Nick's office that day. Josh held Jess's hand firmly in his but that was the only sign that the two were even still together.

Frankie gave Jessica a hug, and her friend happily accepted it.

"Why don't you stay for dinner?" asked Frankie. "I can make something or we can order in."

Jess shook her head. "I have some things to finish at home, and Josh has work to do."

After Frankie and Nick had gotten married Frankie had moved out of the apartment she and Jess had shared. Jess had found a new roommate in Nick's sister Mandy. Josh still had a house in Georgia, where their family lived, but he was renting an apartment to be near Jessica. Both Jessica and Josh had begun attending the church where Nick was pastor.

Mandy rarely attended services at her brother's church. She preferred a church closer to their apartment, and Frankie understood. She knew what it was like to be the preacher's daughter and now the preacher's wife. She imagined that life as the preacher's sister couldn't be a whole lot better.

Frankie helped see Jessica and Josh to the door. When they were gone she turned to Nick. “She looks unhappy,” she said, her tone accusing.

Nick smiled gently and took his wife in his arms. “She will be just fine,” he assured her. “Some subjects in life aren’t easy.”

Frankie almost stomped her foot and demanded that Nick tell her what they were talking about in there. But she managed to control herself and tried to think about something else.

Nick gave her a kiss and told her he had to finish a few things in his office. She gladly let him go. She decided she’d wash the guest room sheets before dinner that evening.

About half an hour later Frankie found herself carefully navigating the stairs with a huge bundle of sheets in her arms. She couldn’t see around the bundle, so she was touching each step with her toes before putting her weight down.

She heard Nick bound up the stairs to help her, and she could see him when he took the heavy sheet off the top of the pile.

“Thanks,” she said, smiling at him.

“Damsel in distress,” Nick teased. “These sheets don’t look familiar.”

“They’re from the guest room,” Frankie explained as they walked down the rest of the stairs together.

Nick laughed. “Are you psychic or do you listen in on my phone calls?”

Frankie gave her husband a puzzled glance. “What?”

“Kyle called a few minutes ago and said he wanted to crash here for a few days. He’s coming tomorrow night. It’s just a funny coincidence that you’re washing the guest room sheets,” Nick explained. Kyle was Nick’s younger brother. As a self-declared professional missionary, Kylie never stayed in one place for long. When he was in the States he usually crashed with a family member or friend, even sleeping a church now and then.

“Kylie’s coming?” Frankie repeated, blinking.

“What’s wrong? You love Kyle.”

Frankie shook her head. “Yes, of course I do. It’s just that my sister, Evie, is coming tomorrow too.”

Nick laughed. “We’ll have a full house.”

“But where are we going to put Kyle?” Frankie asked.

“Good point,” said Nick. “What if I pick up one of those inflatable beds and we can set it up in the spare room upstairs?”

Frankie nodded. That was the right solution. The spare room was large and would make a wonderful space for a child one day but for the moment it was filled with boxes of books and personal belongings that had yet to be unpacked.

"Be sure you get sheets to go with it," Frankie said. She could easily picture her husband driving all the way into town and coming back with just the bare mattress.

"Sheets?" he looked blank. "They don't come with sheets?"

Frankie shook her head. "No, they don't. So please get some. We could also use an extra pillow."

"Maybe you should write this down," Nick suggested.

Frankie kissed her husband, brilliant in so many ways but clueless in others. "I'll make you a list."

Over dinner Nick and Frankie discussed their houseguests.

"I know Evie met Kyle, but I don't think they had time to get to know each other," said Frankie, a forkful of salad on her lips.

Nick shook his head. "I don't know. I was busy marrying the most beautiful girl in the world."

Frankie laughed but was pleased with the compliment. She tried to remember what her older sister, Maggie, had told her about Evie and Kyle. She found that she too had been too wrapped up in the wedding to pay much attention to anything else. “I think Maggie said that Kyle took her for a bike ride. I want to say someone said that she took his bike out without permission but that doesn’t sound like Evie.”

Nick dismissed the idea. “No, that doesn’t make sense. But I’d believe it about your niece!”

Frankie laughed. Her niece, Danni, had only just turned six years old but Frankie had no doubt that the child would steal a motorcycle at any opportunity.

“They’ve met at least,” Frankie declared. “Maybe this will be a chance for them to get to know each other better.”

Nick laughed. “Maybe they’ll fall in love.”

Frankie had to take a sip of water to keep from choking. “Evie and Kyle? That would be quite a match.”

Frankie was picturing tall, dark Kyle with his motorcycle and leather next to her petite and proper sister who always dressed prairie style in an ankle length skirt with her long hair pulled up around her head.

Nick shrugged. “It could happen.”

Frankie laughed. "I see Evie with a more traditional guy. And as often as Kyle travels, I'm not sure a wife and family would be in his future."

Nick had to agree with that. His brother had never settled down and certainly didn't act like he intended to. He lived to travel to poor countries and work to help the people there. Nick didn't see how Kyle could reconcile his passion for missionary work with having a family.

"But I'm sure they'll enjoy each other's company," Frankie said. "And we'll definitely enjoy theirs!"

Frankie was excited the next day as she waited for her sister to arrive. She was hoping the two could spend some time together walking in the park or trying on crazy clothes in the mall. They hadn't done those things in years, and it was high time. They could even invite Jessica along, Frankie thought, and maybe she would confide what was going on with Josh. After that thought Frankie shook her head to clear it. She had to get it into her brain that whatever was happening between Jessica and Josh was none of her business. Still, she wished that Jessica would tell her.

Evie arrived in the early afternoon in a burst of giggles and sisterly hugs. Frankie was thrilled to see her sister, and Evie was looking radiant. Her long hair was pulled back off her face and hung down her back in shining waves. She wore one of her standard jumpers with a scalloped neck shirt underneath.

Frankie smiled, considering her own jeans and button down shirt. She was downright masculine next to her sister.

Nick greeted his sister-in-law and picked up her suitcase. “I’ll take this up to the guest room for you, Evie. Then I’ve got to run out and get an inflatable mattress.”

Evie watched Nick disappear up the stairs and then turned to her sister. “And inflatable mattress? Something wrong with the guest bed?”

Frankie shook her head. “No, it’s just that you aren’t the only visitor arriving today.”

Evie grinned and guessed, “Mandy?”

Frankie led her sister into the living room. “No, it’s Kyle.”

Evie seemed to freeze in her tracks. She stood there, staring at Frankie.

“What’s wrong, Evie? Sit down and I’ll get you a drink,” Frankie said.

Evie shook her head and seemed to come out of her daze. "Oh no, I'm fine. Kyle?"

"You remember Kyle," said Frankie. "He's Nick's brother."

Evie nodded slowly. "Yes. Yes, I remember him."

Frankie concluded that her sister was tired from her long drive and suggested she take a nap. Evie agreed rather quickly and practically ran upstairs to the guest room.

Nick watched her scurry up the stairs as he was coming back down. "Is she okay?"

Frankie nodded. "Tired."

"She moves fast for someone who is tired," Nick observed. He had his car keys in his hand. "I'm going to go pick up that mattress."

"And sheets," Frankie reminded him with a kiss.

"And sheets," he repeated.

Kyle didn't arrive until late that evening. He had told Frankie not to hold dinner for him, but she kept a plate that could be heated.

Evie had gone back to the guest room after dinner, saying she was still worn out from the travel. She seemed nervous and Frankie wondered what was wrong. Frankie was sitting alone in the living room reading a book when she heard Nick open the door.

“Kyle!” Nick gave his brother an affectionate hug. It was obvious the two were brothers. They shared the same facial features and dark hair. However they were different in build. Nick was the older brother but Kyle was taller. Nick was broad with big shoulders and a large chest but Kyle was slim with long legs and a long face.

“Show me to the guest room,” said Kyle. “I’m beat.”

“Sorry, bro, but the guest room is taken. You’re on an air mattress in the spare room,” Nick explained.

“Suits me fine,” Kyle said. “But who has my room?”

Frankie interrupted, entering the front hall to kiss her brother-in-law.

“Lookin’ good, Frankie,” said Kyle with a grin. He held his motorcycle helmet under one arm and a leather bag in the other hand.

“Thank you.” Frankie’s smile was wide. “Are you hungry? I saved you a plate.”

“Good job, sis,” Kyle told her. “I haven’t eaten all…”

Then he stopped and looked up at the stairs. Evie was descending them. Frankie noted with curiosity that she had fixed her hair and was even wearing a little bit of makeup.

“Well if it isn’t Miss Evangeline Caro,” said Kyle. His voice was calm but his face revealed surprise.

“Hi Kyle,” Evie greeted him. “Good to see you.”

“I suppose you’re the one using my bed,” he teased.

Evie shot him a playful glance. “I thought it was my bed.”

“And you are obviously correct,” Kyle agreed. “After all you’re in it, not me.”

Evie and Kyle moved into the kitchen together as if they had known each other their whole lives. Frankie and Nick were left watching them.

“They weren’t like this at the wedding,” Nick said slowly.

Frankie shook her head. Something was definitely going on here.

She shrugged. “I guess I’ll go heat up his food. That’s if he still has an appetite.”

The evening concluded after conversation late into the night, and when the house was absolutely still Evie sat in her nightgown on the guest room bed. She had butterflies in her stomach and a smile on her face as she confidently waited.

Sure enough the door opened softly and Kyle slipped inside wearing nothing but a pair of pajama bottoms. Evie found that she couldn't take her eyes off his strong chest and arms. He moved toward her and kissed her deeply on the mouth. Heat rushed through her body like a lightening bolt.

"Evangeline, what are you doing here?" he asked her.

"This is my sister's house," she replied. "I'm visiting."

"You told me you were staying at your parents house," he said.

"I changed my mind. I needed to clear my head," she said. "And what about you? You were supposed to be in South America right now if I'm not mistaken."

"The plans changed," he told her. "I leave next week."

She closed her eyes and nodded slowly. Kyle took the opportunity to kiss her again. Then he pushed her backwards onto the bed.

"What am I going to do with you, young lady?" he said in a husky voice as he unbuttoned her nightgown. "You know better than to keep me uninformed of your plans."

"You're not my keeper, Kyle," Evie objected, but her voice revealed a shortness of breath.

Kyle pushed his arms up under her nightgown and flipped her over onto her stomach. He pushed the thin fabric away and began to rub her panties. He massaged her bottom with heavy hands and then moved a gentle finger down between her legs causing a short intake of breath.

He smacked her panty-covered bottom hard and Evie hissed. "Kyle! If you wake Frankie up I will never forgive you."

"Shhh," Kyle commanded. He leaned down over her and began to nibble and suck on her neck.

She moaned. "No hicky."

"You're bossy tonight," Kyle told her giving her ear a sharp bite.

"Ouch," she said quickly.

"Well you don't want me to spank you," he said. He bit her again.

The pinching feeling on her earlobe was both painful and pleasurable, and Evie felt the moisture pool between her legs.

Kyle turned her onto her back and pulled her nightgown up over her head. Then he began to stroke her breasts, pulling slightly on each erect nipple.

Evie squirmed and moaned, trying her best to remain as quiet as possible while Kyle went about awakening and seducing every inch of her flesh.

Evie moved her hand to Kyle's pajama bottoms and found what she was looking for. It wasn't hard to find, clearly demonstrating that it was ready for action.

Kyle made a low sound deep in his throat when she touched him. "Oh Evie," he whispered. "I have missed you."

She smiled. She missed him too. She moved her hands slowly and rhythmically until he pushed her away.

"Too much?" she teased.

He growled and bit her on the breasts.

She gasped but then giggled. She was surprised to find that she enjoyed being bitten.

Kyle expertly continued to explore her body while he slipped on a condom.

"I thought you weren't expecting to see me," she said, her voice partially teasing and partially questioning.

He smiled against her naked stomach. "I try to remain prepared at all times for running into you."

She laughed. "Good answer."

He kissed her straight down her body, letting his finger idly stroke her swollen clit.

"I'm ready," she whispered against him.

"Already?" he asked her. She could hear the grin in his voice and knew that it was a cocky half smile.

"Please?" she asked in a high-pitched voice that she knew drove him wild.

He slipped inside of her and began rocking her hard. The bed creaked loudly.

"Slow down," she whispered urgently.

"Too rough?" he laughed.

"Too loud!"

He kissed her on the mouth and slowed his movements but increased the intensity.

She closed her eyes and let herself move with him until she climaxed against him. He followed immediately and the lovers collapsed beside each other on the guest room bed.

"I'm glad you're here, Evangeline," he said.

"Mmm," she murmured still on an orgasmic high.

He leaned over and gave her another kiss. "I've got to go back to my air bed."

She smiled. "I know. I'll see you in the morning."

He kissed her again and then left her there, spent and completely content.

Chapter 4

"Good morning," Frankie practically sang as her sister entered the kitchen the next morning.

"Morning. Where are the boys?" asked Evie. She got the juice out of the refrigerator and began to pour herself a glass. Frankie noticed that her sister was dressed and that her hair and makeup had been done.

"You don't have to do that," Frankie protested, glancing at the juice. "You're my guest."

"So you're an old married lady now and I can't pour my own juice?" Evie teased, giving Frankie a hug.

"Can I make you some breakfast?" Frankie asked her.

Evie made a noise in the affirmative. "So where are they?"

"They went over to the church. Nick's having some trouble with the van, and Kyle said he'd take a look," Frankie sat down next to her sister after putting some bagels in the toaster. "So you know you don't have to get completely dressed before you come downstairs in the morning. Just wear your pajamas or a robe if you're feeling modest. Kyle won't care if he sees you before you get dressed."

Evie's stunned look confused Frankie.

"Are you okay, Eve? I just meant that you can be comfortable at my house."

"Oh no," stammered Evie. "I was just trying to remember if I'd brought my robe."

"You can borrow mine," Frankie told her casually. "So… you and Kyle are closer than I thought."

"The bagels are ready," Evie announced, getting up.

"Sit down. I'll get them," said Frankie. She pulled the peanut butter and cream cheese out of the refrigerator. "So are you?"

"Am I what?" Evie echoed.

"Closer to Kyle than I thought," Frankie laughed. "Are you avoiding this question?"

"Of course not," Evie answered. "We spent some time together after your wedding is all. He's a nice guy. He's funny."

Frankie nodded. "He is pretty funny."

Evie turned toward the large window in the kitchen. "You mind if I take breakfast out to the porch? It's such a nice morning."

“Go ahead,” said Frankie. “I’ll join you in just a minute. I’m just going to do a few things upstairs.”

Evie headed outside while Frankie hopped up the stairs hoping to join her sister.

Frankie took a large trash bag out of the closet and shook it open. She gathered the trash from the upstairs bathrooms and bedrooms. The guest room door was closed, but Frankie knew her sister was downstairs. She opened the door and stepped inside.

She smiled to see that Evie had made the bed. Evie would always be the good girl, she thought. She reached for the trash basket, which was lined with a grocery bag from a nearby store. She began to pull up the handles when something caught her eye.

And then Frankie caught her breath.

There was a condom in the guest room trash.

Frankie blinked for a minute, trying to figure it out. As far as she knew there were no condoms in the house. She and Nick had decided to allow children to come whenever it was time, so they had not used birth control. The only condom Frankie had ever seen belonged to Jessica back in their wild days living at the apartment together.

Frankie sunk down onto the bed. She'd had no married guests in the house. No one had used that trash basket in a long time. Could it have been there before somehow? Could it have been in the house from years ago and somehow Evie had found it and thrown it away in the trash? Nick's mother had owned the house before she got ill, and it didn't seem very likely that she would have a need for condoms.

She looked at it again, not daring to touch it. It wasn't dry or worn as it might have been if it had been sitting in an old house for years.

Frankie sighed. Then she carried her trash down the stairs. She threw it into the large trash can by the side door and then went to the back porch where she found Evie happily humming to herself.

"Hey Evie?" she said carefully making her way up the steps. She seated herself in a rocking chair next to her sister.

"Yes?"

"So I found a condom in the trash can in the guest room," Frankie said quickly.

Evie was silent for a moment. Then she said. "That's weird."

Frankie nodded. "Yeah, that's weird."

The two sisters sat silently on the porch for about five minutes. Evie looked out onto the farmland, just barely able to see the road that ran behind it. Frankie looked at her fingers.

"You're not... um… you don't…" Frankie began but she couldn't quite come up with the words.

Evie looked at her younger sister. "Do you really want me to tell you?"

Frankie's eyes grew wide and her mouth dropped open. She considered the question and then answered, "Yes."

Evie smiled just a little. "You were right before. Kyle and I got close."

"Kyle?" Frankie hadn't even considered who her sister might have been with.

Evie laughed out loud. "Frankie, who else? You think I snuck some guy in the window?"

Frankie shook her head. "No… I just… well you have to admit that it's a surprise, Evie."

Her sister smiled and touched her long hair. "That I will admit."

"And you two are…? I mean he's a missionary Eve," said Frankie.

Evie sighed and shrugged her shoulders. “I know but it just sort of happens whenever we’re together. It’s like we’re being pulled.”

Frankie knew what Evie meant although she had not felt that way about Nick until after they had slept together for the first time, and that had been their wedding night.

“Wow,” said Frankie.

Evie shrugged and crossed her feet. Frankie saw that she was wearing black lace-up boots.

“But why not tell us that you guys are dating? Why be so secretive about it?” Frankie wanted to know.

Evie smiled. “We’re not dating.”

“Oh,” said Frankie. Then she repeated, “Oh.”

“He was supposed to be in South America right now,” Evie told her sister. “How could I date someone who is going to South American for two years?”

Frankie nodded. “But you…”

“It just happens, Frankie,” Evie said. “I don’t know what else to tell you. When we’re together, it happens. He just makes me feel all tingly and alive.”

Frankie nodded and began to breathe a little faster. "The very first time you met?"

"He's made me feel like that since the first day I laid eyes on him when he came for your wedding," Evie admitted.

"But you do have feelings for him? I mean, other than those feelings?" Frankie asked.

"Yeah," said Evie. "But like I said, he's going to South America for two years."

"Well maybe you could go too?" Frankie suggested.

"Funny. That's what Kyle said," Evie mused. "But I don't want to go to South America. I'm just not like that. I like to be at home and to see familiar things every day. I like quiet, not adventure. Kyle and I are just very different."

"He asked you to come with him?"

"Yes," Evie said. "But I said no."

Frankie shook her head. "It's sad. It's like a tragic love affair."

"It's not that sad," her sister told her. "And it's certainly not a tragedy. Maybe I'll just hang around and be his mistress when he visits the States."

Frankie gasped. "I can't believe you just said that!"

“We’re adults here, Frankie,” her sister reminded her.

Frankie nodded. They certainly were.

When Nick and Kyle came back to the farmhouse later that day, Frankie found it very difficult not to let on that she knew the situation. Evie had asked her not to tell Nick and not to show Kyle that she knew. Frankie had never been a good liar. She was pretty sure that Kyle had figured it out by dinner. Thankfully Nick never noticed anything was different.

After they had eaten and cleaned up the little kitchen, Frankie was ready to head upstairs and get ready for bed. The discoveries of the day had made her tired. Evie said she’d go to bed too, but Kyle took her arm.

“Let’s take a walk,” he said. “It’s a nice night.”

Evie nodded. “Sure. If you want.”

Nick told them he’d leave the door unlocked and the porch light on. Evie grabbed a sweater and soon she and Kyle were walking out into the night.

Nick turned to Frankie. “There might be something going on there after all.”

Frankie wanted to tell her husband all about it, but she had to respect that Evie had asked her not to. Besides that, she had no doubt that Nick would disapprove of his single brother and Frankie's single sister having extra-marital sex under his roof. Instead of an answer Frankie just murmured something non-committal.

Leaves and stones crunched under their feet as Kyle and Evie made their way down the old farm road. Very few cars came down this way, and the area stayed quiet for the most part.

"So you lived here?" Evie asked.

"For a while," Kyle said. "I was leaving home pretty regularly by the time I was about fifteen."

Evie was surprised. "Leaving for where?"

"Mission work," said Kyle. "That's all I've ever had a heart for."

"How did you graduate from high school?"

"I went to a Christian school and got credit for some of the missionary work. The rest of the work I did by correspondence," he told her.

"It sounds so strange," she told him. "Most people wouldn't even consider leaving school to do missionary work."

“Most people can only see one path,” said Kyle. “But in truth there are thousands.”

He took Evie’s small hand in his large one and began to steer her to a group of trees. She felt his grip get stronger as they walked along.

When he reached his destination Kyle seated himself on a tree log. Evie stood in front of him, and Kyle looked her square in the eye.

“You told her,” Kyle accused.

Evie sighed. “She found the condom.”

“So you just told her?”

“Kyle, I can’t lie to my sister. She found it, and I told her.”

Kyle smiled at her. “I know you can’t lie. It’s one of the best things about you. But then there are so many best things about you.”

He took her hands in his and Evie felt that familiar feeling of wanting him so bad that her body hurt and loving him so much that her heart might shatter.

Kyle leaned down and put his mouth on hers in an electric kiss that moved to her core. “But you still have to be punished,” he told her.

Once she heard that her whole body perked up with its own electricity.

She shot him a sexy grin. "You were the one who left the condom in plain sight. Maybe you should be getting punished."

Kyle stood, towering over Evie's small frame. He lifted her up off the ground and said, "Oh no, Evangeline. You will always be the one getting punished even if it was me who made the mistake."

He sat down on the log again with Evie in his arms. He rolled her over across his lap and pushed the skirt of her jumper up to her waist. Then he ran his hands over her white panties.

"Panties of innocence," he murmured.

Evie giggled. "You stole my innocence."

He swatted her bottom, leaned down to her face and softly said, "I think it was all an act."

"Ouch!" she said, reacting to the swat. "My innocence was an act?"

He landed ten hard swats on her bottom and had her squirming. "You are definitely not innocent."

"Not anymore!" she said, kicking her feet as he began to spank her hard and fast. Between Kyle's forceful attitude and the pounding on her bottom, Evie found herself wanting to grind against his jeans. He made her so wet.

Kyle stopped spanking her, leaving her bottom glowing with a mild sting. He moved the crotch of her panties out of the way and touched her clit.

She moaned.

"You like that?" Kyle teased. He placed one finger and then another insider her, pushing gently against the tender inner walls of her vagina.

Evie thought she might burst as his fingers began to pulse against the roughness inside her. He brought her to the edge and then removed his fingers and once again found her clit. He stroked it gently and then harder until she was practically bucking over his lap.

"You want to come?" he asked her, his voice expressing his dominion over that particular act.

"Yes," she said. "Please."

He put a little more pressure on her clit and moved it back and forth. Then he circled it, increasing the force a little bit at a time. "Bad girl," he whispered.

Evie came then, her body moving against his jeans and clutching around the fingers he had slipped inside her. Her brain seemed to drain of every thought as she rode the pleasurable waves.

When she was calm, Kyle lifted her up and sat her on his lap. She put her head on his shoulder.

"You want to have sex?" she asked.

"Here? You'd get your clothes all dirty," he told her.

She smiled. "But I want you to get something out of it too."

Kyle tilted her chin up and kissed her hard. "Oh, I do."

Chapter 5

Josh's car pulled into the driveway just as it was getting dark. Frankie was finishing the cooking, and Evie was setting the table.

"I can't wait to see Josh," Evie said. "Let's see… you and Nick, Josh and Jess and Kyle and me. That's six settings. I think I've got everything."

Kyle and Nick stepped through the backdoor from outside. Nick kissed Frankie as they entered. "Where do you want this bread?"

They had been to the bakery to get bread to go with the meal and a cake for afterward.

"Just put it down on the counter. I want to warm it up," said Frankie. She noticed a look pass between Evie and Kyle, and she almost felt light-headed when she saw the passion between them.

She heard the doorbell ring and then the door opening.

"Come in!" she called.

Josh and Jess entered the kitchen, holding hands.

“It’s the soon to be newlyweds,” Kyle exclaimed. He kissed Jess on the cheek and shook Josh’s hand.

Evie kissed her brother and her future sister-in-law. “How are the wedding plans coming?”

“Terrific,” Jess told her. “I’ve got almost everything picked out. I’ll show you some pictures.”

Evie and Jessica sat down at the table to pour over the pictures of various wedding items.

“Frankie, this is what I was thinking for your dress,” Jessica waved a page torn from a magazine. “It would be in blue.”

Frankie hopped over to study the picture. “I love it,” she exclaimed. She looked at her friend and noticed the jacket she was wearing. “I love your jacket, too. Is it suede?”

Jessica’s face colored. “You’ve seen this jacket. I’ve had it for years.”

Frankie shook her head. “There’s no way I could have missed that. It’s new.” Then she saw the look on Jessica’s face and stopped talking.

Josh cleared his throat. “Jess, can I have a word with you?”

Jessica got up from the table and Josh took her hand. Frankie looked at Nick, but his face gave nothing away.

"You can talk in my office," Nick offered.

When the couple had left, Evie looked at Frankie. "What was that about?"

Frankie shrugged her shoulders. "I wish I knew. Let's get the bread warmed up and we'll be ready to eat when they get back.

Josh opened the office door for Jessica and then closed it firmly behind him, clicking the lock. He folded his arms across his chest. "Did you lie to me?"

Jessica shook her head slowly. Then she looked down at the floor. "Yes," she admitted.

Josh closed his eyes. When he opened them they revealed a mix of anger and concern. "Honey, I told you we'd work on this together, but you have to be honest with me."

He held out his hand, and Jessica sighed. Then she reached into her pocket and pulled out her wallet. She handed him a credit card.

"Are there any more?" he asked her, stuffing the card into the pocket of his jeans.

She shook her head.

"There had better not be any more," he told her sternly. "I will not tolerate dishonesty."

"I'm sorry," she told him.

"Are you? Because I've heard that before." Josh was angry, an unusual state for him. He was trying to breathe deeply to control himself.

"You can't expect me not to spend anything," Jessica argued.

Josh grabbed her arm and whirled her around. He delivered a sharp, heavy spanking to the seat of her pants. When he was finished he set her down, crying, in one of the wooden chairs in front of Nick's desk.

"We have rules, Jessica," he told her. "You are supposed to ask me before you buy anything on credit."

Jess sniffed and wiped tears from her face. "But you would have said no!"

Josh took another deep breath. "Those are the rules. You agreed to them, and I am going to enforce them."

"You're treating me like a child," Jessica whined.

"You'd better believe it, honey," Josh countered. "When you act like a child, you can count on being treated like one."

“It’s not fair,” she said. She pulled her knees up in front of her, folding onto herself in the big chair.

“Oh it’s fair,” said Josh, taking a seat on Nick’s desk. “I’m taking on your credit card debt, and I’m going to take control of it. That’s the end of it.”

Jessica looked up at him and sighed. He hauled her out of the chair and flipped her over his leg so that her chest rested on Nick’s desk. Josh yanked down her pants and panties and began walloping her bare bottom.

Jessica shrieked and then tried to suck the noise back in. “What if they hear?”

Josh continued the spanking, Jessica’s bottom yielding to his hand and then springing back with a wobble. Her pale skin began to turn a fiery pink.

“I don’t care a bit if they hear,” he told her. He swatted her thighs and she let out a sob. “You are going to take that jacket back to the store.”

“It was on sale,” she cried. “I can’t take it back.”

"Then you'll pay me for it, and I'll send the money to the credit card. You'll get a spanking at least once a week until it's paid off," he pronounced.

Jessica wailed. "Once a week?"

"At least," he reminded her. He pulled her bottom cheeks up with one hand and slapped the underside with the other until the color was dark and he knew it would hurt when she sat. "You will pay your debts, and your bottom will pay them too."

Jessica cried as Josh continued spanking her until her bottom was a uniform shade of red and just a little bit swollen. He let her stand and then pulled up her pants and panties. When she had finished crying, he led her out of the room. He waited for her outside the powder room while she washed her face and fixed her makeup. By the time they made it back to the kitchen the others were already eating.

"Have a seat," said Frankie. Then she stopped, looking at her friend. "Jess, are you okay?"

Jessica nodded and smiled although it was clear she had been crying.

"Come and help me grab some dessert plates," Frankie said.

Jess followed Frankie into the living room where the china cabinet stood.

"You're planning on using china?" Jess asked, confused.

Frankie leaned close to her. "What is going on? Why were you crying?"

Jess blushed. "Josh spanked me."

Frankie had been on the receiving end of several of her big brother's spankings, and she knew what Jess was going through. "But why?"

"Because I bought this jacket. Please drop it, Frankie. It's complicated," Jessica said softly.

"Because you bought a jacket?" Frankie repeated. "You have a job. You make your own money. You can buy what you please. What is he, a caveman? That's absolutely inappropriate."

"Frankie," Jess tried to interrupt, but her friend was ranting.

"I cannot believe he would treat you like that. What is the matter with him? I'm going out there to give him a piece of my mind." Frankie said.

"Frankie please don't," Jessica pleaded.

At that point, Nick burst into the room. He grabbed his wife by the arm and dragged her outside onto the large porch.

"This is none of your business," he told her sharply punctuating his words with cracks to her bottom.

She hopped. "Ouch! Nick! He can't treat her like that."

"This is none of your business," Nick repeated. He smacked her bottom hard. "You will leave them alone."

Tears flooded Frankie's eyes. "He's too controlling, too hard on her. Can't you see?"

Nick leaned close to his wife. "You do not have all the facts," he told her evenly. "You need to stay out of this."

Frankie's eyes narrowed.

"That's an order, Frankie," Nick said. His voice was hard and left no room for arguments.

"Fine," she told him finally, almost spitting the words. "It's on your conscience."

She flounced back into the house, leaving him standing alone in the night air.

Frankie was furious for the rest of the evening but she managed to be a cheerful hostess until Josh and Jess said goodbye and both Evie and Kyle had gone to bed. At least she'd hoped they'd gone to their own beds.

After her guests were safety tucked away, Frankie moved angrily up the stairs and into her bedroom. Nick joined her a few minutes later.

Frankie put on her nightgown in a huff. Then she went into the bathroom to furiously brush her teeth and wash her face. When she was finished, she climbed into bed and closed her eyes. It was a sign to Nick that she wanted to be left alone.

"Frankie, I'm done giving you time to pout. Snap out of it," said Nick as he was undressing.

Frankie opened her eyes. "What are you going to do, spank me?"

"If I have to," Nick told her. "It tends to work wonders when you are unable to be reasonable."

Frankie shot up. "I am being reasonable. You are the one who isn't being reasonable.

Nick, having stripped down to his t-shirt and boxers, sat next to her on the bed. He looked at her gently. "Sweetheart, I've told you that this is under control. I can't give you the details because that would be a violation of Josh and Jess's trust in me."

Frankie folded her arms in front of her chest. “You think it’s okay that he punishes her for buying clothes?”

Nick shook his head. “Frankie, I’m not discussing this with you. I know you love Jess, but this is not your business. Trust Jessica, trust your brother and trust me. Let this go.”

Frankie fell back into bed and sighed. “I trust you,” she said, “but I’m not happy about it.”

Nick kissed her on the forehead. “Thank you.”

Frankie fell asleep wondering what Evie and Kyle were doing in the guest room.

Meanwhile in the guest room, Evie and Kyle were trying not to make too much noise.

“You sure do come from a spank-happy family,” Kyle teased her as he licked her ear and neck. “Your brother was spanking his girlfriend, and you sister was getting spanked by her husband. I felt left out.”

“It was your brother spanking my sister,” Evie reminded him. She melted against his touch. “And I think they enjoy it in spite of what they say.”

Kyle grinned. “I’m sure they do. But it also serves a purpose, so it’s an especially great idea.”

Kyle began to kiss a trail down Evie’s neck, between her breasts and down her stomach to her sex.

Evie moaned and arched her back.

“Slow down there,” Kyle told her. He licked her, and she giggled.

“Ticklish?” Kyle asked.

“Something like that,” Evie told him.

Kyle rubbed his large hand on the mound below Evie’s stomach. The mass of hair was soft and fine. “You condition this?”

Evie rolled her eyes. “Shut up.”

“I’m going to spank your pussy,” Kyle announced.

Evie bit her lip. “Don’t hurt me.”

“No more than necessary,” he answered. He put his palm over her sex and then brought it down with a gentle slap.

“Mmm,” Evie moaned. It was a feeling she liked. “How could that ever be punishment?”

“Like this,” said Kyle. He smacked her sex hard, and Evie nearly jumped out of the bed.

“That hurt,” she breathed, clamping her legs together.

“I was just showing you,” Kyle said with an evil sideways grin. He slowly parted her legs again.

“Well don’t show me any more,” Evie said. “I’ve been good.”

“Heaven help you if you’re bad,” Kyle murmured. He began to slap her pussy gently, and Evie rolled with the rhythm. The feeling was exciting and calming all at the same time.

When Evie was completely relaxed, Kyle climbed on top of her and kissed her softly. Then he parted her teeth and slipped his tongue into her mouth, just slightly. She opened her lips in response and gave an excited shudder. Kyle pressed himself into her and gently rocked them both to an orgasm.

“You are amazing,” he whispered in her ear. He was still holding her tightly.

She didn’t answer but just cuddled beside him, cherishing his warmth in her heart. She wished she could stay in that position forever and be completely content for the rest of her life.

“I love you, Evangeline,” Kyle said very softly.

Evie pretended not to hear. Unfortunately, she loved him too.

Chapter 6

Frankie stood in the hallway with a duster in her hand. She normally wasn't much for dusting, although she tried to remember occasionally. The spider webs that sometimes showed up on the ceiling were a testament to her lack of attention to household chores when she had other things on her mind.

She had been thinking that Nick's office could use a dust.

Normally Frankie didn't go into Nick's office. It wasn't that he had specifically told her to stay out. It was just that it was his private room to work and relax and that Frankie had never had much of a desire to go inside. Still, she did clean the room now and then, although Nick often did that himself. But she told herself that Nick would like to have his office dusted.

She turned the handle and stepped inside. Nick had gone to the church and Evie and Kyle were off somewhere doing whatever it was that they did. Frankie was alone in the house. And the office needed dusting.

The room was fairly dark except for three large windows on one side. Frankie dusted the bookshelves and the light switch. Then she moved to Nick's desk.

She was annoyed to discover that there were no papers on top. She reached down to the file cabinet and found it locked. She knew that the key was in the top drawer of his desk. That was no secret. She opened the drawer and took out the key.

She studied the shine of the metal and the way the sunlight bounced off of it when she turned it to various angles.

She was thinking about Jessica. Slowly she put the key into the lock and turned.

The file cabinet was full of folders, each labeled with various titles. Frankie dropped her finger into the counseling folder. There she found was she was looking for, notes Nick had taken when talking to Jessica and Josh.

Holding her breath, Frankie pulled out the sheets of paper. Then she put them back in the folder again. Then slowly she lifted them back out and began to read.

When she was finished reading, she slumped back into the chair in shock. Apparently Jessica had accumulated more than $20,000 in credit card debt. Nick's notes detailed conversations with the couple and noted that they had agreed that Josh would take over Jessica's finances until the debt was paid off. Josh was willing to take on the debt with his marriage to Jessica, but he expected her to change her spending habits.

Frankie had no idea her friend had been so irresponsible with money. Frankie knew that Jess bought a lot of clothes, but she assumed that Jessica made enough money at her job to afford it. She had never questioned where Jess was getting the money for everything she bought. Jess had expensive tastes. Frankie had always known that. But how could one person take on so much debt on just clothing and material items?

She realized now why Josh had been angry about the jacket, and she realized why he was controlling Jessica's spending. Nick had been right. It all made sense when she knew the details. But these were details she wasn't supposed to know. Heavy with guilt, she replaced the notes and shut the file cabinet drawer. Then she quickly left Nick's office.

Frankie felt horrible the rest of the day. She tried to focus on housework and then preparation for her Sunday School Class. She found that she just couldn't shake her conscience reminding her how badly she'd behaved.

There was no getting around it. She was going to have to tell Nick. She sighed and seated herself at the kitchen table, trying to figure out the words she would use. He would be angry for sure, but maybe she could soften the news. She looked at the window and spotted two people far in the distance. She squinted a little and saw that it was Evie and Kyle. She put her hand on her chin and chewed on her lip, wondering what it would have been like to give into sexual passion before her wedding like Evie had. She knew that the older they got, the more the sisters were both changing in both their views on life and their ideas of right and wrong. Frankie laughed to herself. That was true except that her sister was okay with what she was doing, and Frankie was still making childish mistakes like letting her curiosity get the better of her.

She wondered what their other two sisters would say about Evie's new hobby. The oldest, Maggie, would likely be shocked. But Claire might understand. She was a missionary, too, after all. So was her twin, Joey. Maybe missionaries just learned to see things in a different light. After seeing so much pain and trouble perhaps they eventually came to the conclusion that life was too short to worry about the morality of individual decisions that didn't hurt anyone else.

Frankie peered at her sister who was seated on Kyle's motorcycle, swinging her legs. Kyle was standing near her. Frankie wondered what they were talking about. She could tell that they were talking, but she couldn't see their faces. Their body language gave nothing away.

Kyle took a deep breath. The cool air stung his throat. Or maybe he thought, that was his heart stinging. "But I love you."

Evie shook her head. "How can I make you understand? It's not about love, Kyle."

He took her hands as she sat sideways on the bike. "Please, Evie. Come with me to South America. We'll do amazing things and make memories to share with our grandchildren."

Evie grinned at the idea of grandchildren, but then she gave Kyle a sad smile. "I don't want to go to South America, Kyle. I would be miserable in South America."

He nodded and looked at the ground. Then he kicked up some dust with his boot. “You want to stay in Georgia?”

Tears sprang into Evie’s eyes. “Yes.”

“Okay,” he said. He paused, thinking. “Do one thing for me? Will you do one thing?”

“Yes,” she told him.

“Pray about it. Pray about it and see what happens. Will you do that?” he asked her, squeezing her hands in his.

“Of course I will,” she told him.

“I’ll pray too,” he said. “I love you, Evangeline.”

He pressed her against his body and she started to cry. She loved him too, but she couldn’t say it. She was afraid she would fall apart.

When they finally came inside, Frankie told Evie and Kyle they were on their own for dinner that evening. Neither of them seemed particularly hungry anyway.

Frankie knew she needed to be alone with Nick, so she drove out to the church to catch him before he came home. He was sitting at his desk typing on his computer when she found him.

“Frankie,” he said, startled at being interrupted. “Is everything okay?”

She nodded. “Yes… well, I mean sort of.”

Nick stood up and came around to the front of the desk. “What’s going on?”

“You’d better sit down,” Frankie said with a sigh. She fumbled nervously with her fingers.

Nick took a seat in one of the heavy chairs in front of his desk and motioned for Frankie to sit in the other. He leaned forward, waiting for her to begin.

“Well… I have to confess something,” she said softly.

“This is a first,” Nick teased. His lopsided grin never failed to melt her heart.

Frankie smiled. “Stop it, Nick. This is hard.”

“Okay, go ahead,” he told her. “I’m listening.”

“I…” she began. She looked up at the ceiling, as if asking God to intervene with an earthquake or some other natural disaster. “I… was doing some housekeeping…”

“Yes?” he prompted patiently.

“In your office,” she continued.

His eyebrows rose. “Well that’s unusual.”

“I sometimes do,” she said defensively.

Nick put up his hands in mock surrender. "Okay, you sometimes do."

She nodded, as if she had won a point. Then she took a deep breath, remembering why she'd come here. "I was curious…"

Now he was interested. He leaned even further forward.

She closed her eyes and quickly spit out the rest before she lost her nerve. "So I looked at your files and read the one about Josh and Jess."

For a moment, Nick sat in silence. Then he said, "You what?"

"I'm sorry, Nick. I just wanted to know so badly," she said, knowing it was no defense. "I couldn't stand that the three of you had a secret from me."

Nick's face was the picture of disbelief. "Those were in a locked drawer."

She nodded. "I know."

"You took the key and opened the drawer, found the file and read it?" he asked her carefully.

She winced. When he said it, it sounded really bad. "It was a mistake," she said.

"Yes, it was."

“I’m sorry,” she offered again.

He nodded his head. “I bet.”

Nick rested his elbows on his knees and folding his hands, pressing his index fingers against his chin. “This is very serious. You invaded Josh and Jessica’s privacy, not to mention mine. You intentionally disobeyed me.”

“I didn’t!” she interrupted. He had never said not to go into the files in his office. He had never said not to read something from his drawer.

His eyes flickered a little, and she involuntarily drew back. “Did I tell you to drop the subject and trust me?” he asked her in a low, threatening tone.

He had her there. She nodded. “Yes.”

“You intentionally disobeyed me,” he repeated. “And you shattered my trust in you.”

That was like an arrow into Frankie’s heart. She started to cry.

“The only thing keeping me from roasting your behind every night for a week is that you came here and confessed,” he said, standing up.

Frankie shuddered. “I know.”

“Go stand in the corner,” Nick said. “I can’t deal with you now. I’m too angry.”

Frankie got up and scrambled to the corner, hoping to avoid angering her husband any more. She stood with her nose to the paneled wall. She’d been in this position a number of times before, waiting to feel the consequences of instigating her father’s wrath. She had hoped that once she’d left her parents’ house she wouldn’t find herself there again. The smell of the paneling reminded her of being punished as a child. Her head swam.

She listened to Nick pacing around the room, and she closed her eyes. She hoped he would take a walk outside to calm down, but he didn’t. Within just a few minutes he was summoning her back to his desk. He was still standing, but he motioned for her to sit down.

She did, and she could feel the weight of her bottom against the chair. She was dreading what might be coming next.

“Okay,” Nick said. “You came to me to tell me about this, so I want to know what you think we should do about it.”

Frankie was surprised. She looked at Nick and tried to determine if it was some kind of test or trick. Then she realized that she knew

Nick well enough to know that he wouldn't play games with her. "What I think?"

"Yes," said Nick. "You know your heart. What needs to happen here?"

Frankie closed her eyes. He wasn't making this easy. But she knew that Nick had a point. If she searched her heart, she would know what would help her to remember Nick's authority and her role as a minister's wife.

"I know I deserve a spanking," Frankie said quietly. "I know it can't be a mild spanking either. I disobeyed you and I deserve to be punished for that."

Nick didn't say anything. He waited for her to continue.

She sighed. "I'll have to apologize to Jess and Josh. You were right. I violated their privacy, and I had no right to do that."

He stood still and watched her, his arms folded across his chest. She tried to think hard about what she should say. She decided to say what was in her heart.

"I know you can't trust me now, Nick, and I'm so sorry. I'm asking you to please forgive me. I will do better in the future, and I will remember to think before I act. Please forgive me, Nicky." At the end of this speech, she burst into sobs.

Nick quickly dropped to her side to hold her and stroke her hair.

"Shh, Frankie. It's okay. I do forgive you," he said softly. "And I will trust you again."

She cried against his shoulder for a few more minutes, and then she lifted her head and wiped her tears away with her hands. "I still deserve a spanking."

"I agree," he told her. "And I think you should let Jess and Josh know that you were punished when you apologize to them."

Frankie blushed, knowing that would be an extremely embarrassing conversation. But she did owe it to her best friend and her brother. She never should have violated their privacy. "Okay," she said.

"Stand up and take down your pants," Nick ordered.

Frankie stood and unzipped her khaki slacks. She pushed them down around her knees. The room felt cold without the fabric against her legs.

"Panties too," said Nick. He was watching her carefully. She wasn't sure if he was trying to make the experience more humiliating for her or if he was looking for signs of rebellion.

Frankie pushed her white rayon panties down to join her pants. She stood there in Nick's office, her bottom bare and her face blazing.

"I am disappointed in your behavior," Nick told her.

She cringed. He was going to lecture her while she stood there with a bare bottom. She felt goose bumps rise all over her body.

"One, you know better than to go snooping in my office. I do not keep personal secrets from you, Frankie, but you are not privy to what happens between me and members of the congregation. That remains true even if those members are your siblings or your friends. Do you understand me?"

"Yes sir," Frankie answered, her eyes falling to the crimson carpet. It reminded her of red bottoms and sacrificial blood. Strangely her father had once had a similar rug in his church office.

"Look at me," Nick directed. It took strength from deep inside for her to obey him. "Two, you violated the privacy of people you love. You act like a child, Frankie, like you think the world revolves around you. I'm here to tell you that it does not. Jessica and Josh have every right to keep personal matters to themselves or to tell who they choose to tell. It has nothing to do with you, and you need to respect that."

She felt her stomach flip. She hadn't thought of it that way, but Nick was right on. What had made her think that she had a right to know Jess and Josh's personal business? She did sometimes feel like she was the center of the universe. "Yes sir," she answered Nick.

"What you did was calculated and deliberate," Nick continued. "It is not as if I left those notes out and you happened to discover them and then read them. That would be bad enough. I should be able to leave private paperwork on my desk and trust you not to read it, shouldn't I?"

"Yes sir."

"But you went into the desk drawer, got out the key, unlocked the cabinet, searched for the papers and then found them and read them. That is first degree disobedience, Frankie, and I am not going to tolerate it."

Frankie felt a tear roll down her face. She was ashamed of herself for the way she treated Jessica and Josh, and she was particularly ashamed of disobeying Nick.

"When I spank your bare bottom, I want you to remember that you behaved like a child," Nick said sternly. "I expect a lot more from you. Got it?"

"Yes sir," Frankie answered again. She didn't dare say anything else.

Nick pulled her to the large desk and then guided her over it so that her elbows were on the polished wood and her bottom stuck up into the air. She was miserable in this position, knowing what she must look like to Nick.

"Stay there," he told her. He returned a few moments later with a hand towel from the church's kitchen. He handed it to her. She knew it was to keep her tears off of the desk calendar that was below her face. He intended to make her cry. She was close to it already.

She whimpered a little as she heard the unmistakable sound of Nick unbuckling his belt and pulling it through the loops of his pants. She shuddered when she felt the leather against her bare skin. Nick was taking aim at his target. He held her around the waist and began swatting her bottom with the belt. He angled the leather so that it would come up and make contact with the lower part of Frankie's bottom. He swung again and again, only slightly varying where he placed the swats.

The unrelenting strikes were too much, and Frankie began to sob. She pressed the towel to her face, letting it absorb her tears. The belt burned her like the sun and she began to feel like she had no skin left on her bottom cheeks. Her face was swollen from crying, and she knew her bottom was as well.

Frankie didn't notice when Nick had stopped spanking her because her bottom hurt so badly that one strike had began to flow into the next. At some point the searing pain in her bottom decreased to a dull sting and she realized that Nick was sitting in the chair behind her.

"That was for forgetting your responsibilities as the minister's wife in this church," Nick told her calmly when her crying had stopped. "You owe it to me, to the church and to yourself to grow up and act like a minister's wife is expected to act."

"Now you're going to get a spanking for your childish attitude and behavior. Come here," he said. She heard him patting his lap. Even the sound of his hand on his own slacks sounded painful.

Frankie stood, her bottom stinging, and turned to her husband. She was hoping to get a break. “Can’t we do this later? It hurts so much already.”

“We’ll do it now,” Nick told her. He reached for her arm and guided her over his sturdy thighs.

She began crying anew as he swatted her sore, swollen bottom.

“You behaved like a naughty little girl, Frankie,” Nick scolded her as he spanked. “You talked yourself into doing something you knew was wrong, and you ignored the feelings of everyone else involved.”

The tears were gushing now, and Frankie felt them on her cheeks, nose and lips. They dripped onto the rug like raindrops off of the trees after a storm.

“Now you’re over my knee getting your bottom spanked like a child, and you will be in this position each and every time you behave like a child. Is that understood, young lady?” Nick was spanking hard, and his words increased the effect of the discipline.

Frankie gasped and tried to answer, but her bottom throbbed and the spanks continued to rain down on her bare skin. She kicked her feet and then thrust them out behind her in an effort to knock the sting away, but it was useless.

"Next time you are going to think like an adult, is that clear?" Nick asked her. "None of this foolishness about needing to know things that are none of your business. You got that?"

Frankie managed an affirmative wail.

"And you're going to apologize to Josh and Jess for what you did to them, and you're going to tell them you got your bottom spanked," Nick declared.

Frankie was crying too hard to protest, and she knew it wouldn't matter anyway. Josh believed in spanking women, and he would have expected Nick to handle Frankie in just this way.

Nick finished spanking Frankie with some hard swats to the places where the belt had fallen, which sent her into hysterical cries. She was still sobbing hard when he pulled her to her feet. He replaced her panties and pants, and the fabric felt rough on her damaged skin.

"I'm sorry," Frankie cried when she could finally form words.

Standing, he kissed her on the top of the head. "I know you are. And I do appreciate that you came to me and told me about this."

Frankie was thanking heaven for that herself. She couldn't imagine what would have happened if Nick had somehow found out about her snooping on his own.

Nick pulled her close. "I don't want to punish you severely ever again, Frankie. Think about your actions before you take them."

She nodded against him, clinging to him. She vowed to behave in a responsible way from that time on, or at least to try her very best.

"I will never, ever snoop in your office again, Nick," she promised.

"I'm glad to hear that," Nick replied. "I need to finish up here but it will only take a few minutes. Is Jess working today?"

Frankie shook her head. "I don't think so."

"Make some calls and see where Josh and Jess are. Find out when we can drop in on them." Nick sat back down at his desk.

Frankie decided not to sit on one of the wooden chairs and instead stood by Nick's bookshelf to call Jessica. Jess was confused when her friend asked to meet them and wouldn't tell her why, but she said that Josh would be at her apartment in just a few minutes and that she and Nick could stop by any time.

Frankie hung up the phone and relayed the news to Nick. He nodded and said, “Let me finish what I’m doing, and we’ll go. In the meantime you can stand in the corner.”

With a sigh, Frankie returned to her familiar spot in the corner of the preacher’s office.

Chapter 7

Jessica opened apartment the door for Josh with a smile on her face and a spring in her step.

“I got paid today,” she announced. She handed him the money to cover the jacket. “That’s all of it!”

Josh grinned and kissed her. “Good girl,” he said. “Just one more spanking for you.”

Jessica groaned and gave Josh a pout. “I thought we were done when I paid it off!”

“We’re done when I say we’re done,” said Josh. He took off his jacket, revealing muscular arms bursting out of short sleeves. He hung the garment on the hook by the door and took Jessica’s hand.

“Is Mandy home?” he asked, looking around.

Jess shook her head. “She’s at work.”

“Good.” He led Jessica into the apartment’s small living room and settled himself on the floral fabric sofa. He pulled Jess over his lap and pressed his large hand to her bottom. She was wearing tight grey leggings that showed off her curves.

"I'm happy that you paid off the jacket," Nick said, patting and squeezing her bottom. "I'm proud of you for that."

Jessica squirmed.

"However, you were dishonest with me. You're still going to be spanked for that," he announced.

He squeezed her bottom cheeks hard, and Jessica yelped with surprise. Then he pushed her leggings down, leaving her bottom covered in a pair of sheer panties.

"You will ask permission before putting anything on a credit card," he told her, his hand still threateningly covering her bottom. "You will not open new accounts. In fact, you will not be going shopping at all for the rest of the month."

Jessica twisted her neck to look up at her boyfriend. "What?"

"You can buy groceries and that type of thing, but you are grounded from the mall and clothing stores," he said.

"That's not fair. I have cash to pay for things," she protested.

He shook his head. "I think you should put that cash toward paying down your debt instead of buying things you don't need.

However, our agreement was that you not create new debt so that decision is up to you after the month is over. Until then you're financially grounded."

She moaned again and dropped her head onto the sofa cushion. She didn't know what she would do with herself if she couldn't go to the mall.

"What if I get a second job? I know they're looking for someone at the mall," she pleaded.

Josh actually laughed. He patted her bottom. "If you really want a second job, I'm not gong to say no. However you will not be working at the mall. You don't want a second job anyway, babe. Do you?"

Jess shook her head. She really didn't. She had just been trying to think of a reason to go into the mall.

"I'm not kidding here, Jess," Nick said seriously, although he was rubbing her bottom in a way that made it hard for Jessica to concentrate. "If this happens again, I'm taking charge of all of your income and putting you on an allowance."

"An allowance?" Jessica wailed. "Don't do that."

“Then don’t break the rules again,” Nick said simply. “Okay, enough talk. It’s time for spanking. I want you to remember this when you’re thinking of buying something on credit.”

He leaned down and brushed her hair aside so he could speak directly into her ear. “And you’d better not ever lie to me again.”

She squeezed her eyes shut as Josh began to smack the living daylights out of her bottom. He quickly got tired of slapping her panties and yanked them down and out of the way. He increased the force of his spanks when he got to her bare bottom, slapping her hard on one cheek and then the other and then placing a volley of spanks where her cheeks met. He repeated this multiple times until Jess was wriggling like a greased pig.

Jess had begun to feel tears threatening to fall when the doorbell rang.

Josh stopped mid-spank. “Expecting someone?”

“It’s Frankie and Nick,” Jess said, her voice breaking.

Josh delivered a barrage of stinging slaps to his girlfriend’s rear end. Then he stood her up and pulled her leggings back up over her bottom. Then he tapped her on the nose with his finger. “You are lucky.”

Josh strode to the door to open it for his sister and brother-in-law. "Come in, come in."

The men shook hands and Frankie kissed her brother. She glanced at Jessica, who was still standing in the living room. "You okay?"

Jess smiled, but her face was red and there were tears in her eyes.. "Yes, I'm fine."

Nick took Frankie's hand and pulled her into the living room. They sat on chairs opposite the sofa where Josh and Jess were seated. Josh had his arm around Jess, and Jess had snuggled in close to him.

Nick cleared his throat. "I just became aware of some information that concerns you both."

Jessica and Josh exchanged a glance and then looked back at Nick.

"Frankie?" Nick prompted.

For the second time that day Frankie took a deep breath and began to tell her story. When she got to the part about the notes, her brother hit the ceiling. Frankie wasn't really surprised. She'd seen her brother react to her antics before.

"You'd better be kidding me, Frankie," he said warningly. For a moment, Frankie thought she was ten years old again.

She shook her head. "I'm sorry, Josh. I wasn't thinking."

Jessica looked sad. Her large eyes searched Frankie's face. "So you know all about it then?"

Frankie nodded. "I'm sorry Jess. I should never have invaded your privacy like that. But why didn't you tell me? I would never have judged you."

Jess looked disappointed in her friend. "I didn't tell you because it's personal, and it's embarrassing."

"What else, Frankie?" Nick asked, looking meaningfully at his wife.

Frankie gritted her teeth. "Nick spanked me for it, hard. And I'm really sorry."

Josh nodded and stood up. "I'm glad he did but with Nick's permission, I'm going to spank you again."

Frankie shrieked and tried to run, but her bother was too quick. He held her by the shoulders and looked at his brother-in-law. "Nick?"

Nick nodded his head. Frankie cried, "I'm too old to be spanked by my brother! Josh, please, I'm a grown woman!"

Josh put his foot on the coffee table and turned his sister over his knee. He was tall enough that her legs didn't reach the floor. She flailed but she knew she wouldn't be going anywhere.

Josh slammed his hand down on her pants ten times fast, and Frankie was crying immediately. Her bottom was still raw from the spanking Nick had given her and this assault renewed the sting. Josh had never been one to hold back when giving a spanking, and this was no exception.

"Are you embarrassed?" Josh asked her, his tone rough. He smacked her again and she yelped loudly.

"Yes!" she told him, her voice a squeak.

"You know that you embarrassed Jessica by snooping in her private matters," her brother scolded, making his point by slapping her bottom with gusto.

"Yes!" she yelled. "I'm sorry!"

"Now you're a little girl getting spanked over your brother's knee," Josh said. "And now you know how you made Jessica feel."

Josh swatted her several more times on her bottom and thighs and then left her standing by the coffee table, tears streaming down her face. He stood in front of her, arms crossed and eyes sharp. "You learn your lesson, little sister?"

She nodded sadly. "I'm sorry Josh. And Jess, I'm so sorry. I hope you'll forgive me."

Frankie's spanking had caused Jessica to cry and she sniffed with a laugh. "Of course I will, Frankie. I love you."

Frankie and Jessica hugged each other, and Nick stood up to shake Josh's hand.

"We'll get going now," said Nick. He pulled Frankie with him out of the room. "You coming over after church on Sunday?"

Josh nodded. His anger seemed to have calmed after he had spanked his sister. "Well bring the pizza."

Frankie gave Jess a final hug before following her husband out the door. Josh kissed Frankie on the cheek and whispered, "I love you, kid. Don't ever do this again."

Nick was quiet as they drove back to the church where Frankie would pick up her car.

"Are you still mad at me?" Frankie asked cautiously.

Nick started. "Sweetheart, no. I was just thinking."

"About what?"

"Well, you know Josh makes a good living. He'll be able to pay off Jess's debt pretty quickly and once they're married he'll be able to give her those designer shoes and high-end clothes that she likes."

Frankie nodded. It was true. Her older brother had built his own business and had found success, although money had never been his primary motivation.

"Frankie, you know I'm never going to make a ton of money. Do you ever wish you could have those things that Jessica wants?" Nick asked, his voice concerned.

Frankie tried not to laugh out loud because she didn't want Nick to think she was making fun of him. She quickly answered, "Nicky, no. I love Jess, but I'm not like her. I don't need $300 jackets or expensive clothes. I've never had those things, and I've never wanted them. I'm perfectly happy just the way we are."

Nick smiled. "I love you, baby."

"I love you too."

Frankie's bottom still throbbed when they got back to the house, but it was nothing compared to the guilt she had been feeling earlier. Now that awful churning in her stomach had been replaced by a glow in her heart as well as in her backside. She knew that Nick loved her, and she had been absolved of the horrible misbehavior from earlier. She was also secure knowing that Jess and Josh were okay, even if that getting that information had been painful. She couldn't be happier.

Frankie and Nick found Evie sitting alone at the kitchen table. She was slumped over an uneaten bowl of ice cream.

"Where's Kyle?" Frankie asked gently, looking around.

"South America," said Evie glumly. She rested her chin in her hand. "I went for a walk and when I came back, he was gone."

"Gone?" Frankie repeated. "Just gone? How do you know?"

"He took his stuff," Evie said. "He didn't leave a thing. He didn't even leave a note."

Nick looked questioningly at Frankie, and she shrugged. "He didn't say anything to me."

"Me either," said Nick. He leaned against the refrigerator, thinking. "That's really strange."

"Maybe they needed him suddenly," Frankie suggested.

"It couldn't have been so sudden that he wouldn't have said goodbye. He's planning to be gone for almost two years, after all," Nick said.

Evie burst into tears.

Chapter 8

On Sunday morning Frankie was ready for church bright and early. The sun was up, the air was clear and she was feeling like she would accomplish a lot that day. She had prayed long and hard, and she had something important on her mind.

When she, Nick and Evie arrived at the church, Frankie excused herself and said she'd meet Evie in the sanctuary in time for services. Then she went looking for Mrs. Dell.

Evie found her in the front hall and asked her quietly if they could talk alone. Mrs. Dell looked wary, and Frankie could feel the stares of other church members on her back. Everyone seemed to know what had happened between her and Mrs. Dell. She wondered exactly how much they knew.

"Please?" Frankie asked quietly. "Can we please talk?"

Mrs. Dell nodded curtly and followed Frankie into one of the Sunday School rooms. A large, brightly colored poster of Noah's Ark decorated the room. Mrs. Dell sneered at it.

"Mrs. Dell," Frankie began, when they were alone. "I want to apologize for my behavior toward you. I have been praying about it, and I am so sorry. It was rude and childish of me to speak to you that way. Can you forgive me?"

Mrs. Dell looked suspicious. "I suppose your husband told you to say this to me?"

"No ma'am," Frankie answered honestly. "He doesn't even know I'm talking to you."

Mrs. Dell blinked and stared Frankie down. "I do not approve of you."

Frankie nodded. "I know. I wish I could change your mind."

The older woman sat down in the teacher's chair at the front of the room. "Before your husband came along we had a wonderful pastor."

Frankie knew that the last pastor at Abington had been a widower in his 80s who had held the position for quite some time. He had died not long before Nick had been offered the job at the church. "Tell me about him," Frankie said.

She pulled up one of the children's chairs and managed to stuff herself into it.

Mrs. Dell pursed her lips, and Frankie could clearly see the red lip liner and clashing smeared pink lipstick she had used. She supposed that Mrs. Dell didn't see as well as she once had. Frankie thought she was about to shut down. But the Mrs. Dell said, "Fred was a good man."

Fred? Frankie took note that Mrs. Dell had called the man by his first name. That was a very unusual way for someone to speak of a pastor, especially an elderly pastor.

"He had no children, you know," Mrs. Dell continued. "His wife had been dead for twenty years. She died of breast cancer."

"I didn't know that," said Frankie. "Did you know her?"

Mrs. Dell nodded. "I did. She and Fred were friends of mine and my husband's. After Laura died, Fred became very sad. He and I were close."

Frankie opened her eyes wide when she realized what Mrs. Dell was saying. "You mean, you… you dated?"

"Certainly not," said Mrs. Dell primly. "We went to the theatre together, and I often made him dinner. People my age do not date."

"Sorry," said Frankie quickly.

"They tried to get him to retire, but he wouldn't. He loved his work," said Mrs. Dell sadly.

"You must miss him," Frankie said carefully.

Mrs. Dell smiled. Frankie wasn't sure she had seen that before. "Yes, I do."

Frankie looked up at the clock. "The service will begin soon," she said. "Would you like to sit with my sister and me?"

Frankie hadn't expected the old woman to agree. She always sat in the same pew three rows back and to the right of the alter, and as far as Frankie knew she'd been sitting there since she was a newlywed.

"I will sit with you and your sister," said Mrs. Dell. "Thank you."

"Thank you," Frankie replied, opening the Sunday School room door for the older woman.

Frankie's smile lit up the whole church as she walked into the sanctuary with her new friend.

That afternoon Frankie, Jess, Josh and Evie stood in the church hall after services had ended and everyone else had gone home. Nick was in his office tying up a few loose ends, and Evie was talking to Josh about the family. Jess pulled Frankie aside.

"Will you go to the drugstore with me?" she asked quietly. "If you say you need to go, then I won't have to worry about Josh coming along."

Frankie raised an eyebrow. "What are you going to buy, Jess?"

Jessica shook her head and smiled. "Don't worry. It's a legitimate expense. I'm just kind of embarrassed to go with Josh." She lowered her voice even further, and Frankie strained to hear. "I have to pick up birth control pills."

Frankie groaned and thought of Evie. "You too, Jess?"

"Me too what?" her friend asked, her face curious.

Frankie forced a smile. "Never mind. I mean, I know you're not a virgin but I thought you and Josh were going to wait until you were married."

Jessica's face flushed. "Oh, we're waiting. The pills are just to get my period stable before the wedding. I don't want to be on my period for the wedding or the honeymoon."

Frankie opened her mouth to respond and then closed it again.

"Frankie?" Jess asked, putting a hand to Frankie's forehead. "Frankie, are you okay?"

Frankie had just realized that she couldn't remember when she'd last gotten her period. "You know, I think I need something at the drugstore, too."

When they got back to the house that afternoon, the half-baked pizza Josh had picked up was in the oven. The two women could smell it from the porch.

"Do it now," Jessica said with excitement as they burst through the door.

"Do what now?" called Nick from the kitchen.

"Nothing!" Jess called. Then she whispered, "Go. Do it now."

Frankie hurried up the stairs, the bag from the drugstore crunching against her legs. Quickly, she shut herself in the bathroom.

A few moments later, she called down the stairs. "Nick! Nick, can you come up here please?"

Nick shot a curious glance at Jess, who was all smiles.

"What's going on, Jess?" Josh asked, putting his arm around her.

"I don't know yet, but hopefully we will soon," Jessica answered cryptically.

He went up the stairs to find Frankie.

"I'm in the bathroom," Frankie called.

Nick opened the bathroom door and found Frankie seated on the edge of the bathtub. She had something in her hand. She showed it to him.

"Is it a thermometer?" he asked her. "Are you sick?"

She shook her head and grinned. "It's not a thermometer. It's a pregnancy test."

Nick's eyes grew large. "Is it… are you…?

She nodded and screamed, "Yes!" Then she flew into his arms.

Nick carried her into the bedroom and set her carefully on the bed. "Honey, did I spank you too hard the other day? I didn't know. Are you okay? Can I get you something?"

Frankie laughed. "I'm fine. Let's go downstairs and enjoy the pizza. I want to tell everyone the news."

Nick's face was full of concern. "Are you sure you're okay to go downstairs? Shouldn't you stay in bed?"

"You want me to stay in bed for the next, what, seven or eight months?" Frankie asked him, laughing.

He shook his head. "No, no I guess not."

He took her hand and helped her out of bed. Then he carefully followed her down the stairs, his hand outstretched so she wouldn't fall.

They found the others in the kitchen. When Frankie entered, Jessica asked, "Well?"

Frankie nodded and Jessica whooped, "Ya-hoo!"

Josh looked at Evie, who shrugged. "Are we missing something?"

"We're having a baby," Frankie announced, her face nearly hurting from smiling.

A cheer rose up from both Josh and Evie who went quickly to hug their sister.

"I'm gonna be an aunt," Jessica exclaimed.

Evie had her arms around her sister. "I'm going to be an aunt, again," she said, referring to their older sister who had two children. "But this time is just as exciting as the first!"

Frankie could see in her sister's eyes that she was wondering if she would ever be a mother herself or if she would have to be content being an aunt for the rest of her life. Frankie hugged her sister tightly, praying that God would give her everything she wanted.

The doorbell interrupted the celebration. Nick went to answer it.

"Kyle?" Nick's voice floated into the kitchen from the front hall. "We thought you were in South America."

Evie stopped mid-hug and slowly pulled her arms away from Frankie. She met her sister's eyes. "Kyle?" she mouthed.

Frankie shrugged. "Do you want to go upstairs? I'll distract him."

Evie shook her head and put on a defiant face. "No. I want to know what he has to say for himself."

Kyle and Nick joyfully pushed through the kitchen door. Kyle had his bag over one shoulder and was wearing his motorcycle gear.

"I need to talk to you," he said to Evie without even greeting everyone else.

"So talk," said Evie defensively. She was still angry at him for leaving without notice, and she wasn't planning to let him off easily.

Kyle looked around the room, assessing whether or not to try to get Evie alone. He decided against it.

"Here," he said. He put a piece of paper in her hand.

Evie read the piece of paper slowly and then shook her head. "Evangeline Ministries?" She looked at Kyle. "What is this? It looks like a lease?"

"It is a lease," Kyle told her. "I've leased an office a few miles from your parents' house. I got an apartment too. I'm giving up missions. Instead I'm going to run an office coordinating missionaries and mission projects. It's all worked out. I'll still have to be away a few weeks each year, but that's all. I named it after you, Evie."

Evie was still confused. "I don't understand. What are you saying?"

Kyle dropped to one knee. "I'm saying marry me, Evangeline. I love you and I don't want to be without you. Please marry me. Will you?"

Jessica gasped, and Frankie started to cry. Evie stood motionless for a few tense moments. "Would you be happy giving up missionary work?"

"Evie, I will be happy only if I can be with you," Kyle told her. He rose from his position on the floor. "We can live next door to your parents if you want. We can live with your parents if you want. I don't care as long as I can have you. You are all I need."

“Then I say yes,” said Evie, and she fell into his arms.

Never had six happier people enjoyed pizza at a farmhouse kitchen table. Josh and Jess, soon to be married, gazed into each other’s eyes and shared dreams about their future. Nick and Frankie talked only of their child and what he or she would become. Evie and Kyle fed each other pizza, Kyle snapping seductively at Evie’s fingers.

The future was bright, and life was good.

www.ingramcontent.com/pod-product-compliance
Ingram Content Group UK Ltd.
Pitfield, Milton Keynes, MK11 3LW, UK
UKHW041935190726
13854UKWH00004B/1604